Promissory Payback

Laurel Dewey

This is a work of fiction. Names, characters, places, and incidents either are the product of the author's imagination or are used fictitiously. Any resemblance to actual events, locales, organizations, or persons living or dead, is entirely coincidental and beyond the intent of either the author or the publisher.

The Story Plant
The Aronica-Miller Publishing Project, LLC
P.O. Box 4331
Stamford, CT 06907

Cover design by Barbara Aronica-Buck
Author photo by Carol Craven

ISBN-13: 978-1-61188-007-6

Visit our website at www.thestoryplant.com

First Story Plant Paperback Printing: July 2011
Printed in the United States of America

PROLOGUE

Detective Jane Perry took another hard drag on her cigarette. She knew she needed to quiet her nerves for what she was about to see.

Another victim. Another senseless, gruesome murder that she would add to the board at Denver Headquarters. When Sergeant Weyler called her half an hour ago, she hadn't even finished her third cup of coffee. "This one is odd, Jane," he told her with that characteristic tone in his voice that also suggested an evil tinge behind the slaying du jour. "Be prepared," he said before hanging up. It was a helluva way to start a Monday morning.

As Jane drove her '66 Mustang toward the crime scene in the tony section of Denver known as Cherry Creek, she tried to look on the bright side. If she'd still been a drinker, she'd be battling an epic hangover at that moment and doing her best to hide it from Weyler. But since becoming a friend of Bill W., her addictions involved healthier options such as jogging, buying way too many pounds of expensive coffee and even briefly joining a yoga group. She stopped attending the class only because the pansy-ass male instructor wasn't comfortable with her setting her Glock in the holster to the side of her mat during class. Since she was usually headed to work after the 7:00 AM stretch session, Jane was obviously carrying her service weapon. She wasn't about to leave it in her car or a locker at the facility. Nor would she be so careless as to hang it on one of the eco-friendly bamboo hooks that lined the yoga room.

So for Jane, it was obvious and more than natural for the Glock to lie next to her as she attempted the Salutation to the Sun pose and arched into Downward Facing Dog. In her mind, there was no dichotomy between the peacefulness of yoga and the brain-splattering capacity of her Glock. As the annoying, high-pitched flute music played in the background—a sound meant to encourage calmness but which sounded more like a dying parakeet to Jane—she felt completely safe knowing that a loaded gun was inches from her grasp. The other people in the class, however, *did* have a problem, and they showed it by arranging their mats as far from Jane as humanly possible. None of this behavior bothered Jane until the soy milk–chugging teacher took her aside and asked her to please remove the Glock from class. Since Jane wasn't about to take orders from a guy in a fuchsia leotard who had a penchant for crying at least twice during class, she strapped her 9-mm across her organic cotton yoga top and quit.

That's what predictably happened whenever you shoved a square peg like Jane Perry in a round hole of people and situations that don't understand the *real world*. Crime has a nasty habit of worming its way into the most unlikely places—churches, schools, sacred retreats and possibly yoga studios. The way Jane Perry looked at life, yoga might keep you flexible but a loaded gun kept you alive so you could continue being flexible. She knew what it felt like to be the victim of circumstance, to be held hostage by another person's violent objective. Even though it was a long time ago, she'd never wash the stench from her memory. Her vow was always the same: *Nobody would ever make Jane Perry a victim again.*

CHAPTER 1

But somebody apparently *had* made the old lady inside the Cherry Creek house a victim. Jane rolled to the curb and parked the Mustang, sucking the last microgram of nicotine from the butt of her cigarette. Squashing it onto the street with the heel of her roughout cowboy boots, she flashed her shield to the cops standing at the periphery and ducked under the yellow crime tape that was draped between the two precision-trimmed boxwood shrubs that framed the bottom of the long, immaculate brick driveway.

Jane checked the front door. There was no sign of forced entry. Stepping back, she searched and easily found two security cameras. **PROPERTY PROTECTED BY S.O.S.—SECURITY ON SITE** the decal read. One camera was poised above the front door and the other located at the corner of the house directed toward the rear of the property. Entering the home, Jane gazed at the gleaming marble floor that gracefully skirted the entry. A French reproduction crescent-shaped walnut wood table stood to the left with a Waterford vase atop it filled with nine strikingly fragrant stems of Oriental "Stargazer" lilies. Jane leaned closer and took a deep whiff of the aromatic flowers. She figured they were damn near fresh due to the sturdy wax coating still remaining on the petals. The heady scent was alluring and certainly disguised the stink of death, urine and fear that awaited her up the magnificent marble stairway and in the master bedroom. Jane steadied herself, fastening her armor around her heart so she'd be able to view what she was about to witness without losing whatever was left in her stomach of the pad thai dinner from the previous evening.

"*Evil requires the sanction of the victim*," she said to herself, recalling the line from *Atlas Shrugged.* It was a powerful statement and one that Jane was too often reminded of when she viewed the battered and often unrecognizable corpse at a violent crime scene. The way she interpreted Ayn Rand's words, in order for a murderous act to take place, somewhere in the chain of events, there *had* to be compliance by the victim. That compliance didn't have to be conscious. In fact, it was usually *unconscious*. But the adage that you attract to yourself what you put out rang true for Jane, no matter how politically incorrect that belief was. Whether it be naively allowing the wrong people into your life or putting yourself in situations that are rife with nefarious outcomes, the one who is labeled the "vic" on the sheet down at Headquarters, usually made some lapse in judgment that allowed evil to take them out of this world in a black body bag.

Sergeant Weyler met Jane just outside the bedroom suite door. Inside, she could see the flash of a camera documenting the crime scene. Several CSIs lifted prints.

In the far corner of the room, a street cop sat next to a petite woman who looked to be in her early seventies. The moonfaced woman stared aimlessly at the carpet, seemingly detached from the grisly scene just twenty feet away.

"What do we know so far?" Jane asked Weyler.

"Not much. Except it sure as hell wasn't a suicide."

Jane was familiar with gallows humor, but Weyler wasn't normally one to participate in it. When she walked further into the bedroom and saw the body, she realized his comment was meant more as a statement of the obvious.

There on the king-size bed was a woman, early sixties, nude, lying on her stomach and hog-tied. Her mouth and nose were taped shut with several pieces of duct tape. One eye was still slightly open and seemingly staring at Jane from across the room. The fear and understanding of death was still imprinted on the woman's orb. Her body may have been cold but somewhere in that shell, Jane felt as if this victim was still transmitting the last impressions she took in before the specter of death choked her final breath. Jane could taste it in the air—the freshness of madness and chaos.

"Her name is Carolyn Handel," Weyler offered. "She's sixty-two and lived in this house for almost thirty years. Her best friend," he gestured tactfully toward the woman seated across the room in the corner, "found her body this morning around 7:30, after getting a call last night from Ms. Handel saying she needed to talk to her. Her name is Laura Abernathy. They've been friends since grade school." Jane shook her head in amazement, partly that anyone could still be friendly with someone they knew for more than fifty years and partly because it was one helluva way to say adiós to your pal.

"Any idea how long she's been dead?" Jane asked quietly.

"Body temp suggests twelve hours."

Jane checked the time on her cell phone. "So about 8:30 last night," she said, more to herself to make a mental note.

Jane moved closer to the bed and viewed Handel's naked body. A yellow stain of urine soiled the white comforter under the woman's pelvis. A smaller mark of feces lay next to her left hip. It wasn't unusual for the vics to evacuate their bladder, since death relaxed the body. But when she saw shit expelled, it often meant that there was a sufficient degree of conscious fear while the attack progressed, allowing to literally "scare the shit" out of them. Across her back, written in red lipstick was **KARMA IS A BITCH!** The lipstick holder sat on the side table, its red phallic crown still exposed to the air, with the dusty trace of fingerprints left around the cylinder by the crime scene techs.

"Whoever did this, took their time, didn't they?" Jane stated. "They wanted her to suffer badly." She looked at Weyler. "Why let God sort it out, when you can take the power in your own hands and make it easy on Him." Jane hunkered down to get level with Handel's point of view. That deathly, terrified stare appeared to be gazing at a point just behind where Jane stood. The only thing in that area was a single chair. "Has that been moved?" she asked one of the crime techs who replied that it was in the same spot when they arrived. "That's an odd place for a single chair, don't you think? Facing the bed like you're watching a TV program."

"Or waiting," Weyler suggested.

"Yeah. Waiting." Jane carefully sat in the chair and looked at Handel. She had to hunker down a bit in the seat to meet the dead woman's fixed gaze. "Waiting," Jane repeated, "to make sure Carolyn saw who was killing her . . . and maybe to make sure she was dead before they left." Sitting there, Jane could almost feel an intangible connection to the ass that sat in that same seat twelve hours earlier. It was right there . . . so close. As if they were still watching Handel suffer the fate they dealt to her.

Weyler noted that the specific knot used to secure Handel was known as a "figure eight." "It's an anchor knot often used in rescues. I believe it's in the Army Field Manual."

"So did the killer want to 'be all he could be'?" Jane took a closer look at Handel's cheeks. They looked puffy, but bloating would take a little longer to cause that. She slipped on a latex glove and gently poked the flesh around Handel's mouth. A soft, crunchy sound was emitted. "There's something in her mouth."

A crime scene tech carefully removed the layers of duct tape. Like confetti erupting from a small tube, strings of shredded paper drifted from Handel's mouth and onto the comforter. Jane gingerly released more of the saliva-laced shreds until she found one strip where she could clearly read the words **Promissory Note.**

"What the fuck—?" Jane muttered. In the background, she could hear Handel's childhood friend, Laura Abernathy, whispering to the street cop. Jane stood up and spoke confidentially to Weyler. "Is there a reason why Mrs. Abernathy is still here?"

"Apparently, she doesn't want to leave her friend."

Jane looked across the room at the round-faced woman. Her diminutive stature was exaggerated by the soft pink dress that hung well below her knees. Clamped in the crease of her elbow was the strap of a matching pink purse. It was the kind of outfit you'd wear to church or high tea.

"Has anyone talked to her yet?"

"Not formally," Weyler stated.

Speaking to witnesses to death at crime scenes was never Jane Perry's forte. Her gruff manner better suited mind-fucking perps in the interrogation room. And when it came to dealing with genteel ladies in pink dresses and matching purses, well, it was anybody's guess what the outcome would be.

After a quick introduction, Jane pulled up a chair so she could be on the same level as Laura Abernathy. She saved her domineering, lording-over stance for criminals. "I'm sorry for your loss," Jane started the conversation. It had become a robotic line all cops used before questioning family or friends of murder victims. There usually was no genuine "sorrow," but it sounded good and usually made the family feel more comfortable when talking to a cop. But Laura's response to her automatic statement was odd to Jane.

"Did you *know* Carolyn?" Laura asked, with a quizzical look.

"No, ma'am."

"Oh. I see. I wondered."

Jane studied Laura. "So, you're saying that you're not so choked up over this?"

"No, that's not what I meant, dear," she said quietly. "I'm just saying that I don't think there's going to many people mourning her loss . . . except those who she owed money to . . . They'll never see a dime from their investments."

Okay. We have a possible motive, Jane figured. And it certainly was in keeping with the shredded promissory note found in Carolyn's duct-taped mouth. "Do you happen to know the names of those investors?"

Laura looked momentarily lost. "Oh, well, no. I stayed out of that. I just know that there were some very angry people who lost a great deal of money because of Carolyn's behavior."

"What kind of money?"

Again, she appeared stumped. "I believe it was about fifty-thousand dollars each." She rolled her eyes. "Carolyn promised them that if they invested their money with her, she'd guarantee them a one hundred percent return within sixty days."

Jane furrowed her brow. "And that quick payout didn't seem a little *odd* to these investors?"

"Oh, sweetheart, I can't answer that." *Sweetheart,* Jane thought. Here was a woman who probably used that term of endearment for everyone she encountered who showed the least amount of interest in her. "I just know that the people involved were all *quite* desperate and the terms probably seemed very attractive to them."

CHAPTER 2

Jane observed Laura. She looked like the archetypal grandmother. The cloying scent of Lily of the Valley and fresh baked cookies was all that was missing. "Did she tell them where she was investing their money?"

Laura cleared her throat. The line of questioning was obviously not something she was prepared for. "Land to build a condo complex near Playa Del Carmen in Mexico. She said she was the middleman for a deal down there and that the return was so high because the developer already had offers of well over two hundred thousand dollars on each condo."

"Did she ever show you photos or blueprints of these condos?"

"Me?" Laura said incredulously. "Why would she show them to me?"

"Well, you're her oldest friend. I just thought that in the course of conversation she might—"

"There'd be no reason for Carolyn to show me that kind of thing. *I* didn't have the money to invest, so why bother?"

Okay, Jane deduced. This was one of those odd friendships—the kind that goes *way* back and continues not necessarily because of kinship but more due to a toxic, familial alliance. Jane considered the state of Carolyn's dead body behind her. If anything screams, "I'm making a statement," it's hog-tying a nude woman and scrawling "Karma is a bitch!" on her back in red lipstick, while stuffing her cheeks with shredded promissory notes. Somebody didn't get their money back, and somebody was mad enough to kill Carolyn Handel because of it. The idea of a ponzi scheme came to Jane's mind. The illegal high-risk investment con was still operating with abandon by numerous get-rich, fraud financiers, even after the Bernie Madoff scandal should have dissuaded these crooks from continuing their disreputable tactics.

"Do you think this condo building in Playa Del Carmen really existed?" Laura looked at the carpet sheepishly. "Do you?" Jane said, as if she were talking to a child.

"I *hate* to say this . . ." her voice was barely audible, "but, no. I don't think it ever existed."

"Then how was she expecting to pay those investors back?"

"I'm not sure. She didn't worry about it. She didn't seem worried about anything, actually. *Her* life was going well." Laura's eyes canvassed the elegant furniture in the room.

So, either Carolyn was a sociopath or just a rotten crook. "Nobody threatened to sue her or call the authorities?" Jane asked, beginning to dislike the hog-tied body getting stiffer by the moment behind her.

Laura let out a sigh. "No. Carolyn had a way of talking to you that made you feel as though you could trust her completely. She carried herself with such confidence. She owned every room she ever walked into."

Sure she did, Jane deduced. Owned it on the backs of other people's money. Jane snuck a look behind her. The crime scene techs struggled briefly to remove the oddly tied rope around Carolyn's ankles and wrists. Rigor was setting in and when the rope was removed, Carolyn's arms and legs were frozen in such a way that she looked like she was about to take flight. Jane turned back to Laura who was staring emotionless at Carolyn's body. She moved her chair to obstruct Laura's view.

"Do you know if she paid any portion of the money back?" Jane asked, in an attempt to regain Laura's attention.

"No," Laura declared.

"You say that with authority. How do you know for certain?"

"Because when I was here, the investors would call and ask her when they were going to get their money back. Some of them were quite agitated. I can't blame them. From what I could hear, time was of the essence for all of them. It's been more than a year since they loaned her the money." Laura's eyes drifted again to the action going on behind Jane. She was seemingly repulsed and drawn to the scene simultaneously.

Jane shifted again in her chair. "What do you mean, 'time was of the essence?'"

Laura froze, biting her lower lip. It was an unconscious reaction that often meant one wished they could take back what they just said. "Oh, well, you know . . ." Laura replied, somewhat struggling to find the right words. "How many people are struggling right now with this darned economy? Time is of the essence for *everyone*, dear!"

Everyone except Carolyn Handel, it seemed. Laura's verbal recovery was somewhat believable to Jane, but there was still something off. "What did she tell these investors when they'd call asking for their money back?"

"She'd always say, '*Oh, darling* . . .' She *loves* to call people 'darling.'" Even though Laura appeared well mannered and sweet, Jane heard that familiar cattiness that creeps out when women of all ages speak badly about other women. But it always sounded somewhat immature for a woman of Laura's age. The cattiness resurrected as Laura adopted her version of what Carolyn sounded like. "'*Oh, darling*, don't you worry one wit! I'll have your money back to you as promised *very soon*. And we'll all be celebrating and be *so* rich!' She was just stringing them along. She was disingenuous to a fault." Laura bowed her head sadly.

"Are you positive that's what she said?"

Laura looked a little irritated at Jane for the first time. "*Yes*. That was her standard response to them all the time! *So* rehearsed, it seemed."

"That must have made you feel uncomfortable?"

"Very much so, Detective," Laura said with emphasis. "I *tried* to . . . gently . . . get through to her that she needed to pay these people back."

"Gently?"

"You couldn't be *presumptuous* with Carolyn. I've known her long enough to understand how she operates."

"And her response to you was—?"

"'It'll be taken care of, Laura!' End of story after that."

"So, what do you think? What did she do with these people's money?"

"Look around this house, sweetheart. *Do you see suffering*? Do you see poverty?"

Jane considered how much Carolyn probably suffered last night as she gasped for air and possibly stared into the eyes of her assailant seated in that single chair as she died. *Suffering.* Yes, that was part and parcel of the vibe behind this one, Jane mused. Look at what *you* have and what I don't have, she figured the perp might have thought.

"How many people invested with her?"

Laura looked at Jane, seemingly frozen once again.

"Are you all right?" Jane asked her.

"Yes. Just tired."

"Do you know how many people may have invested with her and gotten involved in her scam?"

"Oh, golly. I don't know, dear." Laura fidgeted with the sleeve of her pink dress.

"You said they called when you were visiting."

"Yes. Right. I think it was about three."

"Three?"

Laura appeared agitated as if she'd said too much. She let out a sigh. "I think so. Those are lovely cowboy boots you're wearing. Where'd you get them?"

Jane's boots were old, scruffy and far from "lovely." This was the worst attempt at changing the subject she'd seen in years. It was time to vary the line of questioning. Jane glanced over to a framed photo on a nearby table. It was a picture of Carolyn standing in front of an enormous floral display of Oriental "Stargazer" lilies, like the ones Jane saw downstairs. In the photo, Carolyn looked vibrant and quite attractive for a woman in her early sixties. The decomposing body behind Jane belied the beautiful woman in that snapshot. "She liked Stargazers, eh?" Jane asked, motioning toward the picture.

"Yes. They were her favorite flower. No matter the cost, she liked to have them in her home year 'round." The cattiness reignited.

"It looks like she took care of herself."

"Oh, Carolyn *always* made sure to take care of herself."

"She believed in 'me first,' huh?"

"Oh, *yes*." Laura's eyes rolled. "Always has, ever since we were kids. I've known Carolyn since we were six years old."

Laura almost *sounded* six years old when she said that. Jane had to take a moment to figure out how she was going to tactfully express the next sentence. "You're the same age?"

"Yes. Well, I'm actually three months *younger*," Laura said with a proud twinkle in her eyes.

Good God Almighty, Jane thought. She'd pegged Laura at around early seventies when she walked in the room. What kind of hard living had Laura endured to make her look that haggard?

"I saved her life once," Laura offered with a kind of giddiness to her voice, tapping Jane's knee lightly with her hand. "We were on the playground and she had her book bag strapped to her back and secured in front of her with another strap. We were playing on the slide. Carolyn always wanted to show off to the boys, even at a young age. Such a flirt! She was fooling around on the slide at the top and slipped. Her strap got caught around her neck and she hung over the slide, choking. None of the boys she was showing off to moved an inch."

Jane pictured the freakish visual. "What'd you do?"

"I ran up the slide from the bottom and released the hook on the strap which freed her." Laura appeared to be back in time. "She fell to the ground and hurt her knee but she was alive, thanks to me!" She looked at Jane. "Carolyn got *lots* of attention from the boys with that scuffed knee."

Again, with the catty commentary. *This* is why Jane didn't like women in general. Even though she was a card-carrying member of the female persuasion, she hated the bitchy banter and backstabbing that women did to each other. It was even worse when it was shrouded in a sweet sandwich of "friendship," since the claws seemed to scratch with more impunity.

"If you don't mind me asking, Mrs. Abernathy—"

"Oh, sweetie, call me Laura," she said softly touching Jane's hand, "All my friends do."

Right. And I'm your new best friend, Jane mused. Jane deduced that this was how the trap was set between all women—cradle you in the disingenuous arms of familiarity and then hover until you become vulnerable. That is followed by the inevitable pounce and scratching of eyes. Jane tapped Laura's hand. "Okay, *Laura.* Why were you and Carolyn friends?"

Laura gave Jane's question adequate reflection. "She *needed* me," Laura declared. "I was there in her life all these years so she could see manifested before her humility and grace . . . and *gratitude*. You *have* to have an attitude of gratitude, don't you know?"

Oh, shit, Jane thought as she forced a weary smile. She despised trite treacle like that. If this conversation continued in this vein, Jane would need an attitude of fortitude to get through it. "So, Carolyn called you last night and asked you to come over here, is that correct?"

"Yes."

"What time did she call you?"

Laura sighed. The questions were starting to get to her. "Seven-ish. Right before my program was to start."

"Well, you're lucky you had that show. It appears that Carolyn died around 8:30. You could have been here when this went down."

Her eyes fixated on Jane. "Dear God . . ."

"That's ironic, isn't it?"

"Yes. Quite ironic, Detective."

"Tell me a little about your conversation with Carolyn."

"Oh, we didn't talk. When I saw it was Carolyn calling on my little caller ID thingy, I didn't pick up. I wanted to see my program. I figured I'd just come over here this morning."

"I see. So, there wasn't urgency in Carolyn's voicemail message?"

She thought about the question, seemingly detached. "Yes, there was. Quite *a lot* of urgency actually."

"But she didn't tell you why she needed to talk to you?"

Laura's eyes skirted the carpet as if she were memorizing the pattern in the nap. "No."

"Is there any way I can come to your house and hear Carolyn's message?"

"Oh, I erased it, dear. I erase all my messages the minute they come in. But it was a very simple message. She said, 'I need you to come over here a.s.a.p.' She liked to say 'a.s.a.p.' a lot."

Jane knew the next question was probably pointless, but she went for it anyway. "Did you hear any other voices or sounds on the recording?"

"Voices? No. Why would I hear voices on her recording? Oh, dear. I probably shouldn't have erased it, should

I? I'm sorry. But, you know, I wasn't about to jump to attention with her like I usually do. I wanted to see my program."

Jump to attention. Interesting choice of words. "Right. Your program."

"It was on the Family Channel. Do you watch that channel, Detective?"

Jane looked at the sweet, cherubic face of Mrs. Abernathy and wondered why in the fuck she would think that someone like Jane watched the Family Channel. "Not recently," Jane replied.

"Oh, *you should*! It's *so* uplifting to the spirit! This particular show was 'Sharing of the Heart.' It was all about people traveling the world finding what needs to be fixed or changed and making it happen! *Very inspirational.*"

Jesus Christ, Jane thought. Her oldest friend in the world is stiff as a board on a bed not twenty feet away and she's yammering on about The Family Channel and people fixing the problems in this world. "Inspirational."

"'Be the change you want to see in this world.'" Laura said with a soft smile, echoing a quote from Gandhi.

Be the fucking change, Jane mused. She needed to quickly change the subject before Laura tried to sign her up for a peace march. "So you came by this morning?"

"Yes," Laura replied, her face shadowing with sadness.

"How did you get in the house?"

"I have a key. When Carolyn goes away, I come over and water her plants and pick up her mail. Sometimes I dust."

Sometimes I dust? Jesus! The relationship was now clearly defined for Jane. Laura was Carolyn's dependable doormat. "And you saw nothing out of place?"

"No. Nothing." She leaned to the side to catch another glimpse of Carolyn's dead body. "Until I got . . .up here . . ."

Jane moved her chair once again to block Laura's view. "Was the alarm set?"

Laura settled back in her chair, fatigue beginning to show. "Excuse me?"

"The security system? Was it set?"

"Yes. I know the code. I have one minute from the time I enter to get to the keypad and punch in the five numbers that disable it. Same thing in reverse when I leave. Punch in the code and I have one minute to leave."

"What are those numbers?" Jane asked.

"I can't remember. It's based on a word. That's how Carolyn set it up."

"And what's that word, Laura?"

She seemed embarrassed as she leaned forward and quietly revealed the answer. "M-O-N-E-Y."

The rest of the interview, Laura fretted that someone needed to contact Carolyn's only next of kin—her forty-year-old nephew, Joe Harvey—who was out of town in California "talking to a charity." Jane found his phone number in Carolyn's Rolodex and made the call. It was another facet of her job that she didn't excel in. But what was unusual about her quick chat with Joe Harvey was that she got the impression Carolyn's nephew wasn't surprised by the news. "I'm in California on business, but I'll get a plane out today," he told her, sounding rather inconvenienced by his aunt's murder.

Laura was fingerprinted to exclude any prints of hers in the house. She seemed to like the attention she was getting from one of the cops. After her prints were taken, she asked the "nice policeman" who had patiently stood by her side to please take her home. Another cop would follow behind in Laura's old car. Jane thought how Laura looked like a playful pixie as she exited the room, her arm hooked under the "nice policeman's" elbow.

Jane sidled up to Weyler who was talking quietly with a crime scene tech. "Where are the security tapes?"

"They're working on that downstairs," Weyler replied. Jane stared at Carolyn as a tech took close-up shots of the urine stain and feces next to her body. How far can a person fall to end up like this—having their piss and shit photographed? Fucking humiliating, Jane thought.

But that was all part of this ritualistic murder scene. Humiliation. Revenge. Shock. Suffering. *Karma.* People may not remember how you live, but they sure as hell remember how you died if your death was graphic. She turned to Weyler. "Have them copy as much as possible from the tapes that goes beyond last night. I want to see if she's had any visitors."

Jane wrapped up what she could in the bedroom and walked downstairs. She needed a smoke badly. But before she exited the house, she ducked into a small alcove just off the entryway by the table that displayed the odoriferous lilies. One of the techno wizards from DH was reviewing the tapes. "Nothing so far," he offered Jane with a shake of his head. She was about to head out when she noticed a small digital clock on the security panel that housed the two video screens. It displayed 2:00 AM. Jane checked her cell phone. It was 9:30 AM.

"Shouldn't this be the current time?" Jane asked.

The techie agreed, suggesting that there might have been a power glitch since the video he viewed so far showed the correct marker time on the screen. "Once the power goes back on, this clock is set up to start back at 12:00 until it's manually reset."

Jane meandered into the large, chic kitchen and checked the digital time on the stylish oven. It read the current time. Searching further in the house, Jane found another digital clock on a table in dining area. Again, there was the current time. The S.O.S. Security System seemed to be the only unit in the house that had a timing glitch. How convenient.

CHAPTER 3

Jane knew it would take at least a couple days before the Medical Examiner would determine Carolyn's C.O.D. and what was in her system at the time of death. But Jane wasn't about to wait for the M.E.'s report. She needed the names of the investors Carolyn had seemingly conned and the person who might be able to enlighten her was Joe Harvey. After talking to him again on her cell that day, they arranged to meet at his office the next morning.

Harvey owned a downtown Denver consulting firm in a two-story building that incorporated the industrial design that was so popular lately. To Jane, the steel columns and grey-themed palette reminded her of a prison complex. But when she was greeted by the soft splash of water emitting from the indoor koi pond in the lobby and later by the hiss of a handsome cappuccino machine, the prison motif was quickly eradicated. Across the walls of the lobby were more than two-dozen plaques and embossed commendations to Harvey, all pertaining to charitable groups he either directly helped or aided through people who consulted with him. The groups ranged from Veterans associations and hospitals to Habitat for Humanity building programs. Above the plaques were the words **BRINGING PEOPLE IN NEED TOGETHER** in block letters. Carolyn's only next of kin looked like the ultimate networking kingpin.

Harvey greeted Jane in a rushed manner and led her back to his small office. He was all business and seemed like a man with far too much on his plate, mumbling about how he was waiting for a conference call and he hadn't had much sleep. She sat down and offered her usual line to open up the communication.

"I'm sorry for your loss, Mr. Harvey."

"Call me Joe. And don't be sorry." That was the second time Jane's rote statement had been summarily shunned. "Look, I don't mean to be rude or insensitive but my aunt was a despicable human being." He sat down, fuming under the surface. "She lived like a queen off the sweat of her four, wealthy ex-husbands. Going without was not something Aunt Carolyn was into. She *never* gave a dime to help another human being, no matter how desperate they were. Entitlement was her goddamn birthright. She expected everyone to do for her, but she wouldn't do for them! So, excuse me, but her death is no loss to me."

"In other words, you crossed her off your Christmas card list?"

Joe was taken aback by Jane's acerbic retort. "Yes. Very much so."

Jane quickly sized up Joe. He was a tightly wound, intense, no nonsense guy who found his redemption in helping other people. You don't sport the theme-statement,

BRINGING PEOPLE IN NEED TOGETHER, in your lobby for shits and grins. But he also had no sense of humor, Jane surmised. His intensity of purpose prevented wit from shading his life. It was a common side effect she'd noticed of those who dedicated their life to service. It was as though they believed laughter would take away from the seriousness of their endeavors. "So, let's cut to the chase, Joe. Do you know who killed your aunt?"

Joe shrugged his shoulders. "I'm sure a lot of people would want to bump her off!"

"Right. People she owed money to. Do you have those names?"

Joe turned his head to the left and let out a sigh. He absentmindedly fiddled with a red envelope on his cluttered desk. "I have no idea."

Laura Abernathy seemed to have a better bead on Carolyn's unpaid investors than her nephew. "Laura Abernathy said there were three individuals. All in for fifty thousand?"

He looked at Jane somewhat surprised, tension lacing his lips. "Is that right? Three? Fifty thousand?" He leaned back. "Well, I guess my aunt disclosed more to her—"

"Have you and Mrs. Abernathy talked?"

"No. I saw her briefly at Aunt Carolyn's house a couple months ago—"

"She got a voicemail from your aunt the night before the murder. Laura said Carolyn's voice sounded 'urgent.' You have any idea what that might be about?"

He tapped his pencil against the desk. "Knowing my Aunt Carolyn, it could be anything from a stubbed toe to a dripping faucet."

"Which one did you usually respond to?"

Joe looked at Jane, slightly appalled. "Her faucet had to be busted before I'd show up. I learned my lesson well, Detective. That woman never figured out that the world didn't exist for her amusement or needs!"

"I need the investors' names. Based on the way your aunt was found, it looks like an unhappy investor was involved in her demise."

Joe pinched the skin between his nostrils. "Yeah, yeah. I heard." He looked like he was trying to shake the image from his head. "Graphic, wasn't it?"

Jane watched him closely. "So, Joe. Do you have those names?"

As if on cue, Joe turned his head again to the left, exactly as he had done when Jane asked him the same question not thirty seconds before. And then, like clockwork, he touched the same red envelope on his desk. *Tells.* The body gives us all away with those physical and sometimes verbal *tells*. Jane casually glanced to the wall where Joe's attention seemed to be leaning. There were four photos. Two photos featured grade-school children. Another showed Joe shaking hands with a road-ravaged Vietnam Vet and, in the other, a thin gentleman in his fifties who was on crutches.

"No earthly idea," he said, avoiding Jane's glare. Another *tell.*

Jane glanced at Joe's business card. It was a simple white card with grey lettering above his name that read *Founded on Trust—Sustained on Trust.* To Jane, putting the word "trust" twice on your card spoke volumes. "Nice slogan," Jane said, pointing to the card.

"That's not a slogan, Detective," Joe replied somewhat insulted. "That's the way I live my life and run my business." He leaned back in his broken-in, inexpensive desk chair, tapping the eraser tip of a pencil against the layers of papers that cluttered his modest desk. "Without trust, *you have nothing*. I built a reputation on that and I'm proud of it."

Yes, there was that singleness of purpose. "What exactly do you do?"

"I consult with companies and nonprofit groups as to how they can connect with likeminded individuals and create win-win outcomes."

Well, that sentence wouldn't fit on his card, Jane thought. "Why?" Jane asked, catching Joe off guard.

"What do you mean, 'why'?" Joe looked stunned.

Jane decided to play devil's advocate. She didn't have to, but she liked pissing off people like Joe Harvey who were puffed up with self-importance. "Why is it so important for you to help people? What do *you* get out of it?"

Joe seriously considered her question. "My late mother was Carolyn's sister. As rich as Carolyn was, it never trickled down to us. But the one thing that was driven into my head was that it didn't matter how much money you had—the most important thing in life was your word." He leaned forward, mindlessly playing with a paper clip as he spoke. "A man can own all the riches, but he's as good as a pauper if his word isn't his bond. I saw so many people growing up who had nothing, and I knew there *had* to be a way to attract people in need to people with means to help." Joe discarded the paper clip and gave his full attention to Jane. "There is no reason for people in this world to suffer needlessly."

Suffer. There was that damn word again. This guy was the Johnny Appleseed of hope, planting kernels of prosperity in fields where paucity once flourished. Joe Harvey was a take-no-prisoners activist, intent on providing everyone with that elusive "pursuit of happiness." If Joe had his way, there'd be a chicken in every pot, in every home and in every country.

"I've been called a bleeding-heart idealist," Joe quickly added. "I don't give a shit. Nobody should be a victim of circumstance."

Oh, fuck. This was going to be fun, Jane figured. "If there were no victims of circumstance, Joe, I'd be out of a job."

He leaned closer, severity carved across his brow. "*Nobody* should be a victim *of anything*."

Jane felt the resonance of his statement bounce off the walls several times. She decided to go in for the kill. "So how much did you invest in your Aunt Carolyn's little Mexico scam?"

His eyes showed surprise. "How did you—?"

"Laura Abernathy."

"Right . . ." He appeared distracted.

"So, how much did you invest?"

He looked Jane straight in the eye. "Nothing. I invested absolutely nothing on this one."

"This one?"

Joe fiddled again with the paper clip. "After she and her fourth husband divorced three years ago, she asked me for capital to invest in an interactive video game that was being launched in Asia."

"How much did you lose?"

"Not a cent." He shook his head in dismay. "I made a killing." Embarrassment was evident.

"So, Aunt Carolyn wasn't always a crook?"

"I'm not sure. I often wonder if my profit on that deal was made on the backs of others who invested after me in varying 'investments.'"

"A ponzi scheme?"

His face cloaked in sorrow. "Yes. My profit was most likely gained from the misery and loss of another human being's resources. I just didn't understand that soon enough."

Jane nonchalantly stood up and crossed over to the wall with the four photos. She noticed that Joe immediately tensed up. She studied the faces of the men in the two photos. The Vietnam vet's photo bore an inscription reading: "Charley P. Hall, former P.O.W." The other gentleman on crutches was Raymond Honeycutt and he appeared to be from a Denver diabetes support group associated with Denver Health Medical Center. "What were you doing in California, Joe?"

He looked distracted by Jane's attention to the photos. "I went out to L.A. to check out a prospective contact for a new client who runs a children's cancer charity. I wanted to make sure he was legit."

She turned to him. "You physically went to California to check out someone?"

"My word is my bond." The weightiness of his belief system hung around his shoulders. "I had to make sure . . ."

Jane kept her attention on the photos of the two men on the wall. "Make sure about what?"

"You can't be too careful these days. People are getting screwed right and left."

His words felt like daggers. Jane felt an icy shiver race down her spine. She turned to him. "Like your business card says: 'Founded in Trust—Sustained in Trust.'"

"Exactly."

Standing there, she now had a better view of the red envelope on his desk. It bore the emblem of a crown and the word "Travel." "Is that your airline ticket out to California?"

Joe handed the ticket to Jane. "Yeah. Five o'clock flight. Well, we didn't leave the ground for over an hour. It was close to six-twenty actually. There was a baggage weight issue. They had to remove some heavy suitcases and put them on another flight."

"Is that right?" Jane replied. Lots of volunteered information there. *Lots of it.*

"And we seemed to fight wind the whole way," he added, shaking his head.

"So, you were late getting into California, is that what you're saying?"

"Yes. Very much so."

Wow. Scheduled flights and a ticket to prove it. And baggage information that delayed the flight. Jane hadn't seen a guy fight so hard in a long time to prove he wasn't involved in a murder. "A five o'clock flight that left the ground an hour late."

"Hour and twenty minutes at least. What . . . what are you getting at?"

"I'm just counting the hours in my head. Flight left around six-twenty and it's two hours and change to Los Angeles from Denver. So that means you got in around eight-thirty, Colorado time."

"Exactly."

"Wow. That means that, according to your aunt's T.O.D., she was struggling for her last breath about the time you were taxiing down the runway."

"My God," he muttered.

Jane regarded Joe carefully. "Ironic, eh?" She looked at the airline ticket. "Colorado Mountain Airlines? That's about as budget as you can get." Jane recalled how even the bargain airline's logo was economical. It was CMA in nondescript letters with a half-ass illustration of a snow-capped mountain above the *M*.

"My client paid for the trip. Since most of what I do is for nonprofits, I try to cut corners whenever possible."

"Well, Colorado Mountain Airlines fits the bill. They're so cheap, the pilot doubles as the flight attendant *and* baggage handler." Joe regarded her with a stone face. No fucking sense of humor. She noted the travel agency: Crown Travel. The name rang a recent bell. "There's a plaque out front. Something about the Heart Association and Crown Travel?"

"Yes. My travel agent's son was born with a heart defect and needs a lot of medical attention. I do what I can to get the word out." A look of profound sadness overtook him again. "I tried to help . . ." Jane regarded Joe's reaction. It wasn't faked. *I tried to help*. His phone rang and he answered it, asking the person to hang on. Cupping his hand over the receiver, he addressed Jane. "This is the conference call I was waiting for. Would you excuse me?"

"Sure." Jane noted a small seal in the corner of the room: **PROPERTY PROTECTED BY S.O.S.—SECURITY ON SITE**. It was the same company his Aunt Carolyn used. "One second, Joe. Did you know your aunt has the same security system?"

"Yeah. S.O.S. is one of my oldest clients. I arranged it for her. She never did pay me for the install." He arched his eyebrows.

Jane was about to go when she turned back to him. "One more question. I understand you were Carolyn's only next of kin. Were you in her will?"

He sighed soulfully. "I'm her sole beneficiary. Upon her death, I get three hundred thousand dollars." He stared Jane straight in the eye. "And I will donate *every last cent of it* to people who deserve it."

CHAPTER 4

Crown Travel was the size of a postage stamp. When Jane walked in the place, the owner, Jacque Wilde, was finishing up a reservation on the telephone. She motioned for Jane to sit down. Jacque was a woman about fifty with long red hair she wore in a cascade of soft curls. One side of the wall was decorated with cards thanking her for her "fabulous service," while the other wall featured photos taken by her clients of every known vacation destination on the planet. It was evident to Jane from the manner in which Jacque spoke on the phone that she was a hot shot, go-getter with deft abilities to make miracles happen when everyone else would give up.

"Just remember, hon'," Jacque said before hanging up, "flights are like men at a singles' bar—if you miss boarding one, there's usually another available in two hours or less." She hung up and turned her attention to Jane. "Hi, there! Where would *you* like to go?"

"Someplace sunny," Jane deadpanned as she flashed her shield. "Detective Jane Perry. Denver Homicide." Jacque's jaw tensed. "I'm investigating a murder. Carolyn Handel?"

"Oh, of course. Joe's aunt. I saw it in the paper."

"Did you know her?"

"Excuse me?"

Jacque didn't look old enough to have a hearing problem, especially in such a small, noise-free space. "Did you know Carolyn Handel?"

"No, not directly. Just from the occasional mutterings of Joe when she would do something . . . Carolyn-ish."

"*Carolyn-ish*? That doesn't have the same ring as 'pulling a Madoff,' does it? *His* name has become a pop culture term for being financially screwed."

Jacque smiled. "Don't you think 'fucked' is a better word for what Madoff did?"

Jane couldn't help but grin. Jacque was no shrinking violet. She looked up at the wall behind Jacque's desk. There, in block letters and angled on the wings of a jet airplane were the words **WE MAKE TRAVEL HAPPEN!** What in the hell was it with these bold statements of purpose, Jane mused? "You make travel happen, huh?"

"Absolutely! *Here*," she said, handing Jane a business card. "I've got a toll-free number and I'm available 24/7! *And* my commission is lower than any other competing agency in Denver!"

Jane had to reconsider the "go-getter" label she'd silently given her. Jacque had ascended into type A territory that bordered on cutthroat. "How's business been lately? What with the economy and all—"

"It's okay, considering. Hey, two other agencies went out of business in this zip code so that leaves more for me!" She directed her attention to an email that popped up on her screen, read it quickly and then typed a short reply before clicking the send button with a sharp point of her mouse. "You gotta be a fighter these days. But that's nothin' new to me. I've always had to be a fighter. I've been a single mom since Travis's dad skipped out on me when he was six months old. He couldn't handle the idea of having an imperfect child. Men can be such weak assholes, can't they?" Jacque turned a framed photo on her desk toward Jane.

Jane wasn't going to take the female bonding bait, dishing about men's weaknesses. She stared at Travis. It looked like one of those standard yearbook shots. In this one, the boy was standing in front of a tree in a neatly starched white shirt, arms crossed over his chest with a forced smile. He looked weak, somewhat scrawny and lacking the vibrant energy most teenagers give off.

"That's an old shot. But I like it. He's twenty-eight now but he's still my baby boy. We've been through a lot together and we're still goin' strong!"

"Joe mentioned something about Travis being born with a heart defect?"

The comment slowed Jacque down for a second. And it was a quick second. "Yeah. Right. That's what I meant about my asshole ex-husband leaving because Travis wasn't 'perfect.' But I always told my kid that medical doctors would one day figure out how to fix his heart."

"Still waiting, huh?"

"No, they figured it out. A little over a year ago, his doctor told us about an operation that was close to one hundred percent effective. But then Travis lost his job a week later because he was absent so often due to his health. So, of course, he lost his health insurance and I couldn't get *my* fucking insurance agency to sign him up because of his preexisting condition, blah, blah, blah. You know the score, right?" Jacque glanced at Travis's photo with a melancholy eye. "We were *that* close, you know? *That close* to making my baby perfect!"

"How much did they want for the operation?"

"Almost a hundred grand."

Math was not Jane's forte, but it was simple to calculate that a one hundred percent return on fifty thousand dollars equaled one hundred grand. *Ironic*. Fucking ironic. Suddenly, Joe Harvey's sorrowful comment of, *I tried to help* seemed to take on another meaning when he mentioned Jacque's son. It wasn't beyond reason that Joe, being the do-gooder that he was, maybe hooked up Jacque with his Aunt Carolyn in hopes that Jacque could see the same financial windfall that he had experienced. Of course, that may have been before he realized the ponzi profits were coming from future investors that might never materialize.

"How's Travis doing?"

Jacque sighed. "Oh, good days and bad. He works part time. He's back living with me. I thought it was best. I can keep an eye on him if he needs help." She straightened her back. "We're not giving up though! We *never* give up! I keep telling him that if you want to change your life, you gotta *make* it happen!"

Jane pointed to the slogan above Jacque's desk. "You make travel happen."

"Sure as shit do!" she said proudly. There was a thoughtful pause and then, "We're not victims, you know? I won't allow the use of that word in our home. Victims aren't fighters. Victims roll over and let others kick the shit out of them. No matter what happens, *I will never* be a fucking victim of anyone or anything."

This broad wasn't kidding. Instead of her happy travel slogan, Jane concluded Jacque should replace it with Ayn Rand's declaration that, "Evil requires the sanction of the victim." Any fool dumb enough to cross this mama lion would have his testicles hacked and left to bleed out.

Jane quickly switched subjects, discussing the timing of when Joe booked his trip to California. Jacque showed Jane via the computer that his ticket was issued a week prior. Jane walked around her desk to get a better view of the computer screen. "You book all Joe's tickets?"

"Sure. He's one of my oldest and best clients."

"Did he rent a car?"

"No. He flew into Burbank airport and was meeting his client in Glendale. So, he opted to take taxis since it was going to be a quick trip."

"Can't you get him a good deal on a car?"

"Sure! But that's what Joe wanted to do."

"You book his hotel?"

"Of course." She clicked a few keys on her keyboard to pull up Joe's travel itinerary. "He stayed at the Budget Inn right near the airport. It's just two blocks away. He probably walked it, knowing Joe."

"To save his client money."

"Exactly."

Jane leaned against the desk. "God, if there were more people in this world like Joe, we'd have a better world, wouldn't we?"

"You have no idea, Detective," Jacque murmured, scrolling through Joe's itinerary.

It was a statement that seemed extremely loaded to Jane. She waited for Jacque to embellish but the woman suddenly became uncharacteristically taciturn. Jane craned her neck to get a better view of Joe's page on the computer screen. "Any idea when he checked in to that Budget hotel?"

Jacque clicked her fingers across the keypad with lightening speed. "His plane was quite late getting in."

Jane played dumb. "Really? How come?"

"Well, it doesn't tell us on here. Could be weather or baggage issues."

"Baggage issues?"

"Yeah. These smaller planes have extremely strict weight rules."

"Right. Colorado Mountain Airlines. The el cheapo human transporter."

Jacque forced an odd smile toward Jane. For some reason, the woman seemed insulted by Jane's sarcastic remark. She turned back to the computer screen. "What CMA lacks in stature they more than make up for in other ways."

"What other ways?"

"Excuse me?"

Crazy how Jacque's hearing seemed to fluctuate. "How does CMA make up for it?"

She looked Jane straight in the eye. "Impeccable customer service." This time her smile was genuine. She turned back to her computer screen. "They make travel happen just like I do!"

Jacque expressed a need to get back to booking a backlog of clients' tickets. Jane nodded and was about to make an exit when she spotted another photo of Travis on Jacque's desk. It was tucked close to her computer. There was the boy, looking much older, in a more recent shot, standing outside on what appeared to be an airport tarmac. He was wearing a dark blue jacket with a clear emblem on the left breast pocket. Jane easily recognized the economical block lettering and half-ass illustration of a snowcapped mountain above the "M." It seemed that Travis worked for Colorado Mountain Airlines. Ironic, Jane thought. *Fucking ironic.*

CHAPTER 5

"Anything interesting on those security videos?" Jane asked one of the techies back at DH.

"Nothing so far. It's like watching a test pattern," he lazily replied. "I have video of Handel leaving and coming home but that's it for action."

Jane hated depending upon someone else to do follow-up. They usually never had the same interest or keen eye she possessed. "I want to check the tapes out later myself," she stated, picking up the phone.

"How many hours you want cued up?"

Jane dialed. "Every last fucking minute." She connected with the head desk at the Budget Inn where Joe Harvey spent the night. It was instantly clear to Jane that the voice on the other end was that of a brain-dead seat warmer who didn't have a clue. When she asked the guy if he recalled seeing Joe Harvey, he spent most of the time saying, "Ummm" and "Uhhh." The most she could get out of the Mensa reject was that "his computer showed" that Harvey checked in at 9:35 PM. Factoring the one-hour time difference between California and Colorado, that would make it 10:35 PM MST. Even with the flight delay, Harvey should have checked in at least two hours before that. Jane asked to talk to a manager, hoping to get a better bead on the situation. After an interminable time on hold listening to Barry Manilow sing, "I Write The Songs," an older-sounding woman with a bad cough came on the line.

"Yeah, I remember him," the woman said, expelling part of her lung. She described Joe to a T.

"Did he seem agitated?"

"Nah. If anything, he was quite relaxed. Real easy goin' kinda guy. Said he'd been across the street at the Airport Lounge gettin' some food and doin' some readin' and he lost track of the time. That's why he was late checkin' in. Said he was out here on business overnight and was glad to find a hotel so close to the airport. He complimented me on our lobby. Nice guy."

Lots of volunteered information there. *Lots of it.* The same way Joe offered so much "chatter" info to Jane about his plane being late due to baggage issues. It's not that a person can't shoot the shit with a woman behind the counter of a budget hotel. That wasn't the point. The point was understanding the *type* of person who would naturally do that, and Joe Harvey, in Jane's mind, was not that type. People who are out to save the world have a single-minded purpose that prevents them from wasting their time or breath on chitchat that is not driven to their specific goals. They are far too focused on their self-important objectives. And referring to Joe as "relaxed"? Well, again, the intensity that colored him during Jane's interaction with him was not likely to be transformed into "relaxed," especially after a delayed flight and a nocturnal arrival walking to a budget hotel. No, if anything, irritation would be the key word.

It had to be an act, Jane deduced. *A carefully orchestrated act* just in case anyone like Jane followed up on his appearance at the hotel and asked about his behavior. He *had* to make his interaction with the woman at the front desk memorable for her, just in case.

Her mind drifted to the two photos on Joe's office wall that she felt held significance in this whole mess. Pissed-off investors, perhaps? Jane's clear photographic memory recalled Charley P. Hall, former P.O.W., and Raymond Honeycutt from a Denver diabetes support group associated with Denver Health Medical Center. After calling the V.A., it took Jane less than ten minutes to track down Hall. Without Jane being too specific about her visit, he agreed to talk to her that evening at the house he shared with his daughter in Montbello. Raymond Honeycutt was even easier to find, being that he was actually *in* Denver Health Medical Center as a patient. But she was informed that Honeycutt was under "massive sedation" due to "mitigating factors" and probably wouldn't be able to talk to her until the next day. Jane figured Honeycutt was either in the psych ward or dying. Either way, she wasn't looking forward to their visit. Tonight, she'd tackle the former P.O.W.

When Jane pulled her Mustang up to the ramshackle house that night, she made a point to secure her Glock a little tighter against her rib cage. This section of Montbello was no *Ozzie and Harriet* neighborhood, unless Ozzie was a drug dealer and Harriet was his mule. A child's bike lay across the front steps, along with stacks of old newspapers, garbage bags and pots with dead plants. Jane knocked on the door and was about to put out her cigarette when Hall opened the door.

He was a giant of a man, towering around six feet eight inches tall and barrel-chested. A cigarette teetered precariously from his chapped lips, dropping embers onto his well-worn flannel shirt. She swore that one errant ember touched the back of his hand and singed the hair, but Hall never flinched an inch. This was the kind of guy who chewed ammo and bathed in napalm when he served in Vietnam. He still sported his military buzz cut and his blue eyes still spied the Vietcong around every dark corner.

"Mr. Hall. I'm Detective Jane Perry." She started to extinguish her cigarette.

"You can smoke in here. I don't give a shit," he said, ushering her inside.

This was going to be different, Jane mused. She walked into the low-ceilinged house, cluttered from end to end with junk. Between the claustrophobic environment and dim lighting, it felt like a bunker. Several empty bottles of Jack Daniels lay discarded on their side next to an easy chair that had well over two- dozen cigarette burns. Hall lowered his large frame into the chair, momentarily wincing with pain. He motioned for Jane to move a pile of dirty clothes off the couch and sit down.

"Thank you for seeing me on such short notice, Mr. Hall."

"Well, it wasn't like I had anything planned. Just the usual." He withdrew a bottle of Jack Daniels secured in the side of the chair's cushion. "I'm halfway through a fifth of Jack and a quarter of the way through my third flashback of the night."

Jane's protective instincts kicked in. "I noticed the kid's bike outside. Is there a child in the house?"

"No. My seventeen-year-old grandson stole it from a six-year-old Down syndrome kid. He's trying to sell it on eBay. Said he's going to use the money to get his tongue split so he can look like a lizard. He's not here or I'd let you arrest his useless ass." Hall took a generous swig. "My daughter's at work. She waits tables at a biker joint on Colfax. On the weekend, she works the pole at The Pussy Palace strip club. My sixteen-year-old granddaughter is at her Lamaze group. In three months, she'll deliver twins. We've haven't gotten the DNA results back on the four potential boys who might be the father. The fifth possible match won't get out of juvie until after the twins are born. So, life's a real adventure around here."

He took another gulp of whiskey and Jane sucked a hit of nicotine. She knew the answer to her next question but she wanted to hear it anyway. "You move in with your daughter by choice?"

"Oh, yeah. Between the curb appeal and neighborhood potlucks, how could I turn her down?"

"How long have you lived here?"

"Nine months, seventeen days. But who's counting?" He knocked back another swig.

Jane leaned back and felt the stab of metal bite into her lower back. She turned and withdrew a single piercing in the shape of the sun.

Hall shook his head in disgust. "Oh, Jesus." Jane handed it to him. "My daughter is always losing these damn things. Seem to keep falling off her nipples . . ."

Okay, this was obviously a bleak existence for Charley P. Hall, former P.O.W. The Vietcong never tortured Charley as much as his own trailer trash family. Jane took a hit of nicotine. "Why'd you lose your house, Mr. Hall?"

"Who said I lost it?" He was wily even though he was half in the bag.

"You don't live here by choice. Who caused you to lose your house?"

Hall eyed Jane with steely grit as he methodically lit a new cigarette off the ember of the one in his mouth. "*Who*? What do you mean 'who?'"

Jane figured he had a knife in his boot and a gun tucked into his waistband, either one ready to put to use if he felt cornered. She casually unbuttoned her leather jacket to reveal her holstered Glock.

Hall leaned forward. "Your service weapon looks dusty. When was the last time you emptied a clip into a perp's head?"

Jane leaned forward, mirroring Hall's intimidating manner. "This morning. Right before breakfast. Haven't had a chance to clean it yet."

He stared at her for a hard minute. Jane never moved a muscle. Thankfully, he couldn't hear her heart beating like a horse at full gallop. He slightly relaxed and sat back in the chair. "Want a drink?"

Even if Jane were still bending her elbow, she would have declined his offer. "No, thanks. I'm on the job."

"And that job would be . . . what?"

"Finding the individuals who invested in Carolyn Handel's scam."

"What makes you think I'm one of them?"

"I saw your photo on the wall of Joe Harvey's office."

"That's all? A photo? Why would that make you think I was an investor in some woman's scam?"

The alcohol was lowering Hall's ability to tell a lie. As far as Jane was concerned, the guilt of association was all over his face. "Call it intuition. You know what that's about, right? Like when you were in 'Nam and walking through a field and you just knew it was booby-trapped? You just *knew*. I looked at your photo on Joe's wall and I just knew."

He shrugged his shoulders. "What if I did invest with her? What does it matter?"

"Well, for starters, she'd dead."

Hall's face never changed. No surprise. No smirk. No sadness. Nothing. "Okay. And?"

"It wasn't from natural causes."

"I still don't know why you're here—"

"I did a quick check with the County Clerk's office today. The house you lived in for over thirty years went into foreclosure ten months ago. You'd taken a second mortgage on it last year, and you weren't making regular payments." She noted how Hall's eyes narrowed into a menacing glare. Jane calmly continued. "My theory—and it's just a theory of course—is that you mentioned this in passing to Joe Harvey, and he wanted to help you by hooking you up with his Aunt Carolyn who promised to make all your problems go away if you loaned her your last fifty thousand dollars—"

He jerked forward, slamming the Jack Daniels bottle on a soiled carpet. "Do I look like a guy who'd be that stupid?"

"I never said you were stupid, sir—"

"Well, that's what I'm hearing! You think if I had fifty grand, I'd hand it over to some goddamned woman without checking her out? You think I'm a fuckin' fool?!"

Jane studied his face. That's exactly what Charley Hall did. And he hated himself for it. He woke up with that regret, and it was the last thing on his mind before his tired head hit the pillow at night. He thought he was smarter than that, but somehow the booze and PTSD had marred his judgment. But he was sure as hell not about to admit it to some female cop who had the gall to remind him of his desperate decision. Jane felt nothing but sorrow for the guy. He'd be dead in less than five years, she figured; either by eating his gun or the result of his rotting liver. But she also knew that the bile rising up into his throat was putrid enough to fuel the rage and possibly trigger the need to kill Carolyn Handel. Proving that, however, was another thing altogether.

"I don't think you're a fool, sir. I really don't." Jane casually took a final hit of her cigarette before squashing it out in an overburdened ashtray. "I would like to ask you where you were on Sunday night."

Hall drained the whiskey bottle before tossing it to the side. "Same place I am every goddamned night. Right here. In this chair. Under this fuckin' roof. Waiting . . . Just waiting . . ."

Jane nodded. "Okay, sir. I'm sorry to bother you. I just thought that it wasn't out of the realm of possibility that you were victimized by Carolyn Handel." She stood up.

Now it was Hall's turn to study her. "I'm a lot of things, Detective. I'm a drunk. I'm fucked in the head from too many nightmares. I obviously sucked at being a decent father. I'm all that and a lot more. But I am *not* and will *never be* a goddamned victim. You understand me?" Jane held his steely glare as he stood up, slightly unsteady on his feet. "I know what a victim looks like, Detective," he slurred. "I left a field full of them back in that Godforsaken country for the gooks to pick over. I was only able to rescue a few soldiers, you know? That was my job before *I* got picked off by the Vietcong. I did helicopter rescues.

Tied a figure eight around their waist and lifted them up to safety." He stopped. As drunk as he was, he realized he'd said too much.

Figure eight, Jane thought. Just like the knot used to hog-tie Carolyn Handel's body. The ironies were getting just a little too close together.

CHAPTER 6

Jane couldn't sleep much that night. After smoking half a pack of American Spirits and watching another television cop show that she silently picked apart for accuracy, she still couldn't shake the Handel case. Her gut told her that Charley P. Hall was somehow involved in Handel's murder but at the same time, her gut also told her that the picture was still not complete. She'd wanted to review the security tapes from Handel's home but by the time she'd gotten back to DH, the tech had secured them so well that she couldn't locate them. With any luck the M.E. would have something to offer her tomorrow on what was in Handel's system at her T.O.D. Perhaps that info could create more links to a possible suspect.

She reevaluated the interviews in her mind with Joe Harvey, Jacque Wilde and Charley P. Hall, searching for connections between them. There was nothing to join them except Wilde and Hall's need for quick money and the possibility that Harvey may have hooked them up with his aunt. She didn't feel that Harvey was the type who would knowingly get his friends or acquaintances involved in something that was financially dicey. After all, he admitted to Jane, clearly discomfited, that he'd made "a killing" on one of his aunt's "investments." As risky as Handel's "investment opportunities" may have been, Jane felt it was more than probable that Harvey genuinely wanted to help his friends—one with a seriously ill son who needed an expensive medical intervention and one being evicted from his long standing home. It *was* curious, Jane thought, how when she mentioned the word "victim," all three of them reacted strongly. It was as if the word carried odious contempt.

After a night of restless sleep, Jane got into DH early in hopes of viewing the security tapes from beginning to end. But the tech was late getting in, leaving Jane to reconsider her morning routine. She called Denver Health to inquire as to the conscious status of Raymond Honeycutt. "Oh, he's quite awake!" the nurse advised her.

When the elevator doors opened on Honeycutt's floor at Denver Health, Jane understood the not-so-subtle reason for the nurse's statement. Emanating down a long hallway and centered in a specific room, Jane heard the sound of metal clashing together and echoing, angry screams from one pissed-off older man. When she shadowed his doorway, the scene was chaotic. The floor was peppered with four empty orange plastic prescription bottles. Standing in the corner of the room was the likely pitcher of said bottles, Raymond Honeycutt, balancing precariously on his right foot while his left leg was conspicuously missing from the knee down. Jane was certain he still had ownership of that left leg in the photo on Joe Harvey's office wall. Honeycutt held his cane out with his right hand, jabbing at the trio of nurses and orderlies who stood five feet from him. In his left hand, he held the metal cover that protected his most recent uneaten meal. Using the cover like a shield and the cane like a sword, Honeycutt held the medical staff at bay, the whole time screaming bloody murder.

"I can't take the pain!" he shrieked, his eyes wild. "You tell me it's phantom pain? *Bullshit*! Let 'em cut off your leg and see how it feels!"

Jane recalled that Honeycutt was a member of a diabetes support group. Guess that wasn't going so well.

"Mr. Honeycutt!" the male orderly yelled, "get back in bed please! You have reached your limit of pain medication!"

Jane leaned down and retrieved an empty orange bottle from the floor. It was Demerol, a strong narcotic painkiller that was allegedly in the drug cocktail that killed Michael Jackson.

"*I'm dying of pain here*!" Honeycutt screamed, thrusting his cane toward a nurse as beads of sweat formed across his forehead.

Jane recognized Honeycutt's behavior as what occurs when an addict is withdrawing from a drug—the manic eyes, the sweat, the often-incoherent rants and the real sense of physical pain that is born from the vicious craving of the body for another hit. She pulled out her badge and flashed it in the air. "Mr. Honeycutt! Please calm down!"

Honeycutt strained to focus on Jane's badge. "What in the hell? You called the cops on me?!"

"Sir! Sir!" Jane exclaimed moving closer to his bed. "They didn't call me. I came here on another matter. Would you put down the cane and the . . . catering cover, please. I really need to talk to you."

"Get me a Demerol and I'll give you five minutes!"

"Give him a Demerol," Jane instructed the nurse.

"But, he's already had—"

"I need to talk to him! Give him a fucking Demerol!"

The nurse shot daggers at Jane but complied and then headed out with the others, after whispering, "You don't have to deal with the son-of-a-bitch."

The drug seemed to take effect quickly, allowing Honeycutt to lie back in his bed, surfing the temporary wave of drug-induced anesthesia. This would be the second interview Jane had done in less than twelve hours with individuals who were wasted. Not knowing how long Honeycutt might be conscious, she decided to omit the introductions and go straight to the jugular of her visit.

"Mr. Honeycutt, do you know Carolyn Handel?" He looked at Jane, his eyes mere slits, and said nothing. "*Mr. Honeycutt*? Carolyn Handel! Do you know her?"

"Fucking bitch," he mumbled.

"So, that's a 'yes?'"

"Worthless piece of shit," he said, nearly incoherently.

"I need a 'yes' or a 'no,' Mr. Honeycutt."

His eyes opened wider and he looked at Jane with menace. "*Yes*," he clearly replied, vitriol seeping from his lips. He pointed toward his amputated leg. "She's the reason I had to get that cut off! And that bitch is the reason I'll probably lose the other leg too!"

"You loan her money? Fifty grand?"

"*Why*?"

"Answer my question."

He looked at Jane with a surly, evil expression. "I don't have to answer shit! Nothing you do to me is any worse than what I'm going through right now!"

"You mean, like arrest you? Why would I have to arrest you? I asked if you loaned her money. Not whether you killed her." A look of surprise was followed by a sweet smile of satisfaction on his face. "You didn't know that she died? She did. And she suffered." His smile turned into a sneer. Jane purposely worded the next sentence carefully. "Nobody will ever again be a victim of Carolyn Handel like you were."

Honeycutt reached out and grabbed Jane's sleeve. His strength belied the drugged out stupor he was quickly speeding toward. "*Fuck victims*!" he whispered. "Like that saying goes, 'There comes a time when you better decide whether you're hanging on the cross or banging in the nails.'" His eyelids fell like lead and he lost consciousness. As far as Jane was concerned, she was staring at the third and final investor of Carolyn Handel's latest scheme.

She left Honeycutt's room and returned to her Mustang. Jane felt the gathering of clues coming together in a loose, yet still imperceptible quilt of understanding. Her cell phone rang as she sped away from the hospital's parking lot. It was Sergeant Weyler. The M.E. had made a preliminary finding on Carolyn Handel's tox report. She had enough Demerol in her bloodstream at the time of death to choke a horse.

Ironic.

CHAPTER 7

Back at DH, Jane headed directly to the audio/video room to view Handel's security tapes. While the tech assured her that the tapes "showed nothing out of the ordinary," she waved him off and cued the video to the earliest point available, which was seventy-two long hours prior to the crime. It was tedious to watch the dual video of Handel's front and back door. Jane slowly advanced the video, stopping it periodically to check the time code on the bottom of the screen and then continued the slow fast-forward motion. She watched Carolyn walk in and out of her house several times, only using the front door. Never once did the woman appear to look freaked out or anxious. If anything, she carried herself exactly as Laura Abernathy said, as if she "owned the room."

Two hours passed and Jane's eyes grew blurry, but she maintained her sentinel pose and continued to watch nothing happen. And then something finally did happen.

Joe Harvey could be seen walking up to the front door carrying a huge bouquet of flowers that looked like the Stargazer lilies Jane spotted in Carolyn's entryway. She recalled how aromatic and fresh they were on that morning. Jane paused the video and checked the date and time code. It was Sunday afternoon at 2:45, which was two hours and change before Joe's flight to California. This was strange behavior for Joe Harvey, Jane mused. If she was correct in her assumption that Joe felt badly about getting his friends involved with his aunt *and* based on his own obvious disgust at Carolyn's cavalier attitude, what in the hell was he doing bringing her a large bouquet of her favorite flowers on a Sunday afternoon? Jane resumed the video playback and watched as Carolyn answered the door and clasped her hands together in a show of happiness when she saw the flowers before ushering Joe inside.

And then Jane waited. And waited some more. The guy had a flight to catch at 5:00 PM, which meant he needed to be at DIA by 4:00 PM. On a Sunday with no weather problems or rush-hour traffic to factor into the equation, Jane figured it would take about forty-five minutes from Cherry Creek to get to DIA, park your car, board the shuttle to the main concourse and check in. This meant he needed to leave his aunt's house by 3:15. Why was he showing up with her favorite flowers at 2:45, knowing he had to book it in less than half an hour? Sure, it could have been done on purpose to give him a reason to make the visit brief. But, again, given Joe's overt hatred of his aunt's behavior, why bother?

The tape continued to roll as Jane pondered the possibilities. She leaned back in the chair as the minutes lapsed. What did she know for certain? Well, Carolyn loved Stargazer lilies so much so that a photo of her in her bedroom featured the aromatic flowers. Okay. What else did Jane know for sure? Carolyn was arrogant and believed the world revolved around her. She *loved* attention. According to Laura, Carolyn nearly hung herself on her book bag strap on the slide because she was showing off to the boys. So, putting these few pieces together, Jane let her mind wander into possible scenarios. *If* Joe had exchanged a few salty conversations with his aunt in regard to paying back his three friends, she might not have been eager to meet with him. But perhaps he knew how easily she could be manipulated by simply bringing her a stunning bouquet that she couldn't resist? That would get him in the door. But what did they talk about for thirty minutes, given Jane's determination that he had to be out of there at 3:15 to make his flight?

Jane turned her attention to the clock on the wall. She'd been drifting in thought for nearly forty minutes. She looked at the video screen but there was no sign of Joe leaving. Irritated, she fast-forwarded and then stopped to check the time code on the bottom of the screen. Something suddenly didn't make sense. She fast forwarded again and stopped, checking the code. It was identical to the last one. Hitting the play button, Jane moved closer to the video screen. It was suspended. Asleep. Frozen.

Jane quickly reversed the tape to the point where Joe arrived with the flowers. Resuming the playback, she focused only on the time code, watching it count the seconds and minutes until it halted and the picture froze. "Holy shit!" Jane exclaimed. She figured she knew exactly when it was going to "wake up" and sped fast forward until the time code reactivated at 7:30 AM, the moment that Laura Abernathy entered the house and told Jane she punched in Carolyn's code to deactivate the alarm. What she actually did, it appeared to Jane, was *reactivate* the security system. This was starting to add up. Jane recalled that when she ducked into the security alcove off Carolyn's entryway on the morning of the investigation, she noticed a small digital clock on the security panel that displayed 2:00 AM. The techie told her that there might have been a power glitch and that once the power goes back on, the security clock on the panel would resume at 12:00 AM. Since two hours had passed at that point, it fit that Laura's entrance into the house was the mitigating factor. Jane's theory was born out when there was no video of Laura arriving at Carolyn's house that morning but plenty of video of cops entering the front door, along with Weyler and Jane's appearance.

Jane checked the time code on the active video. It seemed that it had a fail-safe internal memory since it "woke up" with the correct time. Jane had no clue how to suspend a security video and she was fairly sure that Laura Abernathy didn't either. Rolling back the video, Jane found Joe's arrival with the flowers. It took another seventeen minutes before the video froze. Time enough for Joe to get inside, maybe schmooze with his aunt and then disappear into the alcove while she arranged the flowers in her Waterford vase. It wasn't outside the scope of possibility since Joe owned the same security system. S.O.S. was his oldest client, according to Joe. "She never paid me for the install," he grumbled to Jane. Could Joe have possibly been involved with the installation of the system, thereby allowing him a better understanding of how it worked and the various functions it was capable of doing? Whatever the truth, it was too much of a coincidence that Joe's arrival and the suspension of the security system occurred simultaneously. It led Jane to wonder about other possible videos she'd like to view—videos showing passengers departing on Colorado Mountain Airlines planes.

By the end of that day, Jane had seen and heard all she needed to create the possible scenario that led to Carolyn Handel's death. While all the pieces weren't in place, there were enough to formulate her next move. She waited until the following morning to implement it.

CHAPTER 8

Jane arrived at Laura Abernathy's small home at 9:30 AM, parking her Mustang two blocks away. She made a quick call on her cell phone, feigning urgency in her voice that she hoped would be believed. A nervous edge crept up as she squashed her cigarette on the pavement and walked up the modest pathway to Laura's front door. A large *G* hung to the right of the door. "God," maybe? She rung the bell and Laura answered, still dressed in her nightgown and robe. The woman looked even older than when she first met her on Monday morning. What was it with the way Laura Abernathy seemed to age?

"Detective!" Laura said with a warm smile. "Did I forget a scheduled meeting with you?"

"No, ma'am. I was in the neighborhood and I thought I'd stop by and see how you're doing. May I come in?"

Laura's eyes twinkled, clearly adoring the attention. "Well, of course!"

It wasn't just hot in Laura's house. It was "grandma hot"— the kind of stuffy heat one associates with one's grandmother when her circulation starts to slow to a crawl. "What does the 'G' stand for outside?" Jane asked.

"Gratitude!" Laura replied, joining her hands in a prayer pose. "We must have an attitude of gratitude, detective!"

"Of course," Jane nodded. "Carolyn didn't have that, did she?"

"She sure didn't!" Laura's mouth turned up quickly. "I'm sorry the place is a bit of a mess. I just haven't felt up to cleaning lately."

The place wasn't just a mess; it looked like somebody turned the tiny house on its end and shook it hard. Newspapers piled up on the kitchen table next to junk mail next to dirty plates. It was as if Laura had given up trying to create order in her existence. As Jane walked around the tiny, suffocatingly hot living room, the imprint of energy was that of a woman who wasn't all there mentally and physically. It drastically contradicted Laura's carefully coiffed appearance at the crime scene, with her pretty pink suit and matching purse. "Please have a seat, Detective."

"Could I use your phone? My cell phone battery gave out."

"Oh, of course." Laura pointed to a tiny desk brimming with even more paperwork. "I'll make us some peach tea." She scurried into the kitchen.

Jane crossed to the desk. She had to remove several piles of papers to find the phone. Next to the phone was the caller ID box. Jane skimmed through the numbers and names, most of which were doctor's offices. She checked well past the previous Sunday before replacing the papers back over the phone. Jane craned her neck to make sure

Laura was still occupied in the kitchen before examining several of the pages. They were from various doctors, reminding her of her next appointment. Returning to Laura's kitchen table, Jane took a seat, after removing several blankets from the chair.

"Would you like a little honey?" Laura asked, taking an inordinate amount of time to put the tea bags in the cups and pour the water.

"Sure. Are you feeling okay, Laura?" Jane's voice was atypically quiet and subdued.

"Oh, not really," she said, absently stirring the honey into the cups. "I'm so cold lately."

Jane checked the time on the kitchen clock. She needed to speed this up. "Let me help you with those." Jane got up and carried the cups of tea to the table, removing more debris from another chair so Laura could sit down.

"You are the sweetest policewoman I've ever met."

Jane took a sip of tea. "Yeah, I hear that a lot. So, Laura, remember when you told me about that inspirational program you watched on the Family Channel? The one you didn't want to miss when Carolyn called you? 'Sharing of the Heart?'"

Laura looked at Jane, her smile still present. "Yes. My program."

"People traveling the world finding what needs to be fixed or changed and making that happen?"

Laura sipped the tea. "Yes. That's right. Oh, did I put too much honey in your tea?"

"I wanted to watch the show," Jane continued, staying on track. "So, I checked to see when it was going to be on again. But I found out that no such show ever aired on the Family Channel. No such show by that name aired *anywhere*, in fact."

Laura scratched her head. “Perhaps it was a video. Yes, that’s what it was. I get these things confused sometimes.”

“If it was a video, it wouldn’t have prevented you from going to Carolyn’s house that night when she called and left that urgent message.”

Laura took another sip of tea and smoothed the drape of her robe. “I don’t understand what you mean,” she said quietly.

Jane gently pushed the teacup aside and leaned forward. “Carolyn never called you last Sunday night. I checked your caller ID box just now. It holds fifty numbers and goes back two weeks and she’s not on there once.”

“Really? How strange.”

“I got a preliminary report yesterday regarding the fingerprints we found in Carolyn’s bedroom.”

“Oh?”

“They all belong to you.”

“Well, of course, I’m at her house a lot—”

“They are all over the lipstick container. The one you used to write ‘Karma is a Bitch!’ on Carolyn’s nude back?”

Laura’s smile melted into a disapproving frown. “Well, I see where this is going. I thought you were my friend, Detective. How fickle people are these days!” Her countenance became suddenly hard. “You do things for them all your life and all you want in return is a little ‘thank you,’ or gratitude. You have to have an attitude of gratitude, you know?” Her twinkly eyes stared at Jane with a steely glare. “You’re no different than . . .”

“Than Carolyn?”

“Yes. What? Are the two of you secret friends?” That cattiness that Jane detected when she first interviewed Laura reemerged.

The doorbell rang in quick successive tones. *Right on time*, Jane thought.

"Good Lord! Who is *this*?" Laura grumbled as she struggled to get up and cross to the front door. Jane got up and walked quietly to the opposite side of the door, away from view.

The doorbell was still ringing as Laura opened the door. Joe Harvey stood there looking frantic.

"*Laura*! You and I need to talk!" Joe asked Laura, his voice pitched up several octaves.

"What's wrong, Joe?" Laura asked, confused by his appearance.

"I got a call about fifteen minutes ago from a desk sergeant at Denver Police saying that you had been over there yesterday, talking about Carolyn's case and sounding erratic—"

"No, I couldn't have been there yesterday. I was at the—"

"*Laura*," Joe interrupted. "Remember how we talked at length about the importance of *staying on message*?"

"Yes, yes, of course . . ." Laura looked at the floor, seemingly detached. "I'm so confused, Joe. First she shows up and then you . . ."

Jane slowly opened the door wider. "That was me who called you, Joe. I sucked a few heavy hits off my cigarette to make my voice sound good and raspy. Come on in." As frenzied as Joe had just been, he suddenly became oddly calm and reserved. "Have a seat," Jane suggested to both of them, motioning toward the cluttered kitchen table.

CHAPTER 9

Jane pulled up a chair and sat six feet across from them. Distance was always a good idea in situations like this. "'Staying on message,' huh? You actually believed Laura could do that, Joe? You've known her longer than I have, but I figured that one out from day one. *Finally*, Laura was getting the attention she'd always wanted, instead of that selfish bitch Carolyn!" Jane looked at Laura. "When you constantly put yourself in a subservient position, it's kinda nice to get a taste of what the queen enjoys. Am I right?" Joe reached over and cupped his palm over Laura's shaking hand. "So, of course, you're gonna talk . . . and talk . . . and talk."

Jane directed her next remark to Joe. "I know that bothered you. When I was going over my time with you in your office, I noticed how you tensed up when I told you that Laura mentioned about the three investors putting in fifty thousand each. That was not for public consumption." They remained silent. "I'll take that as a 'yes.'" Joe stared at Jane, his upper lip quivering. "But, Joe, you actually gave yourself away before that. You told me you'd 'heard' about how your aunt was found and how 'graphic' it was. But then you stated that you and Laura had not talked in two months. So, *she* didn't tell you about Carolyn. And Homicide didn't disclose it to the media. The only way you knew what Aunt Carolyn looked like in her last hour on this earth is because you were there."

"I showed you my airline ticket," Joe declared, still unmoved.

"Yeah, that was a very nice cover operation you pulled off. You needed investor number one, Jacque Wilde, to help you with that." Joe's mouth tensed. "And she was *all* about making that travel happen! *You* bring people together to invest and make money and *she* makes travel happen, *especially* when she doesn't get her money back." Jane leaned forward, resting her elbows on her knees. "But *I* can make video happen. I made video happen at Aunt Carolyn's house and I made it happen yesterday at DIA when I asked to see security footage of passengers getting on that five o' clock Colorado Mountain Airlines flight last Sunday. All I had to do was use the *T* word—*Terrorist*—and I could watch all the video I wanted as soon as I wanted to see it. And I got to see it all, Joe. *All of it.* I got to see you heading onto the tarmac for your five o' clock flight. I also got to see Travis Wilde, Jacque's kid. You know, the one who got fucked out of his heart operation and who needed one hundred grand to pay for it? Yeah. I got to see Travis in his distinctive CMA jacket walk out the door right after you and then, about five minutes later, all the way back down the hallway you can see him returning through another doorway pushing a covered cart. Unfortunately, there are no distinct camera angles showing what happened on the tarmac. But, my theory is, he got into an elevator alone with that cart and when those doors opened, two people got off the elevator. One left DIA and headed to Cherry Creek and the other, went back to that five o'clock flight to make sure the 'baggage weight issue' he created earlier would detain the flight as long as possible. I guess that's what Jacque meant when she told me what CMA lacks in stature, it more than makes up for in customer service."

"You've got quite the creative little mind there, Detective."

"Yeah, well, stay with me. If you think that's good, you'll love the rest of the story." Jane cleared her throat. "So, I'm not sure who picked you up at the curb. But I'm betting it was Laura. The two of you needed to show up together at Aunt Carolyn's front door. Of course, we don't have the video of that because you made sure when you delivered the flowers earlier in the day to put her video transmit on 'sleep' mode. I'm not sure how you explained your reappearance to Carolyn. Certainly, she must have been a little suspicious to see you twice in three hours, being that you weren't cozy pals. But I'm sure you flattered her and encouraged everyone to have a drink. And while one of you kept her occupied, the other one slipped the Demerol into her glass." Laura turned away, looking off to the side in a distant stare. Jane studied her. "Really? *You* did it, Laura?" Laura's mouth twisted into a nearly undetectable smirk. Jane turned to Joe. "How many pills did Raymond Honeycutt have to cheek? Four? Six? You think he adequately weighed the pleasure he would get from knowing he helped kill Carolyn versus the stark realization that going off his pain meds cold turkey would send him into an addictive hell? Oh, what am I talking about? He was dedicated to the cause! A good solider in your vengeful army.

"But then, there's another soldier in your party. A *real* soldier. I'm not sure when or how Charley P. Hall showed up to the execution, but it was fairly soon after you two did. Oh, he *really* wanted to be there. He'd lain in bed too many nights in that trailer trash dump of his daughter's, dreaming of ways to eviscerate Carolyn Handel. *But,* he couldn't show up with you. That much I presumed. He hates Carolyn more than he hates the Vietcong, and you needed to get Carolyn whacked out on Demerol first so she wouldn't fight him or call the cops."

Jane shifted in her chair. Laura's attention was still remote, drifting and detached. Jane eyed Joe. "You and Charley carried Carolyn upstairs, followed by Laura, and went about the job at hand. I'm sure the hog-tying was Charley's idea. He loved that figure-eight knot, and he'd probably been fantasizing about ways to incorporate it into this event. Everybody wore gloves, expect for you, Laura. I mean, why bother, right? You're there all the time doing Carolyn's bidding. Watering plants . . . picking up her mail . . . dusting . . . It made sense that your prints would be all over the place. I'm not certain, though, whose idea it was to stuff her mouth with shredded promissory notes and tape it shut—"

"Mine," Laura said, suddenly reconnecting with the conversation. "That was my idea."

Joe looked at Laura aghast. "Laura? What are you doing?"

She patted his hand in a reassuring manner. "It's all right, Joe. I was prepared for this to happen." Laura looked at Jane. "I stuffed her mouth. I taped it shut." Her voice was cool and casual, as if she were ordering take-out.

"And then I saw the lipstick and I just *couldn't* resist." She shrugged her shoulders and smiled like a little pixie—a twisted pixie, but a pixie nonetheless. "Karma *is* a bitch," Laura stated. "And so was Carolyn." She sighed with relief. "It feels *good* to get this off my shoulders. I forgot to take the lipstick container when I left. Silly me."

"And when you left, neither Joe or Charley were there," Jane added. "At least Joe wasn't there. He had to get to DIA to make his eight o'clock flight on Colorado Mountain Airlines." Beads of sweat formed on Joe's brow. "It's that damn video again, Joe. As much as you tried to obscure yourself, I still picked you out of the short line boarding that eight o'clock flight. Not to mention, a clear view of you speeding through the security checkpoint at 7:35."

"I'm the one who killed Carolyn, Detective," Laura declared with a proud cadence. "I'm the one who pulled up that chair and watched her die. I made her look at me. Right in the eye."

Jane recalled sitting in that same chair just days before, strangely feeling a close, yet intangible connection to the posterior of the person who watched Carolyn suffer. Back at Carolyn's house, Jane felt like whoever committed the crime was still watching Handel suffer the anguish they'd dealt. And Jane was right. Because, at that time, Laura Abernathy was seated behind her wearing her pretty pink dress with the matching purse and flirting with the nice policeman, while sneaking glances at her murderous handiwork on the bed.

"Waiting." Jane added. "How long did you wait?"

"Hour and a half," Laura recalled. "Maybe a little longer. She'd go in and out of consciousness in the beginning.

Oh, it wasn't like we didn't talk during that time. Well, I was doing the talking. She was doing the grunting."

"What did you talk about?" Jane asked.

"I told her that she was going to die and that she just had to accept it. I told her that those people she stole money from needed their money back desperately. And the fact that she didn't care or feel any compassion for their struggles was the reason it had ended up like this. But I looked in her eyes, and I could see that even with death approaching, she had no remorse for what she'd done."

"How about you? Do you have remorse for what *you* did?"

"None," Laura offered. "If she'd just . . ."

"Just what?"

"If she'd just been more grateful in her life for what people did for her . . . I saved her life, Detective. She would have died on that playground slide when we were children. She would have hung herself on her book bag if I hadn't run up the slide and unhooked her strap and freed her." Laura cocked her head with a mystified gaze. "She never said 'thank you.' *Never.*"

"You killed her because she never said 'thank you'?" Jane asked.

"In a nutshell, I guess I did. I figured she was alive only because of *me*. So, if anyone was going to take her out of this world, it should be *me*. Completes the circle, so to speak."

So to speak, Jane thought. "How did it finally end?"

"She was unconscious for a while. And I was getting a little sleepy myself. So, I figured I'd just put the tape over her nose. She was dead in a matter of minutes." Laura stroked the felt belt on her robe. "Remember that program I told you about, Detective? 'Sharing of the Heart?' I did see it somewhere a long time ago. And it always stuck with me. People traveling the world finding what needs to be fixed or changed and making that happen. I could be on that show. I found what needed to be fixed and changed and made it happen."

It had been a while since Jane interviewed a criminal that was as cold and calculating as little Laura Abernathy, this fragile, physically weak, rapidly aging woman. Jane stood up and pushed her chair against the table. She glanced at Joe who hadn't said a word for some time or moved a muscle. "I get it. Really I do. Carolyn was a capital *C*. A narcissist who only thought of herself and lived off the sweat of others. But you don't kill those types of people. You turn them in. You get the authorities involved."

"Oh, Jesus! Give me a break," Joe muttered, ending his self-imposed silence. "Trust me. I looked into it! The authorities aren't interested in cases like hers unless you can *prove* she siphoned millions. Ever since Bernie Madoff, they only want the big guns. Not the small-timers like my Aunt Carolyn. And I don't know for sure, but I think she knew that. Fifty thousand here, fifty there . . . stay under the radar—"

Jane ran her fingers through her hair. "You *still* don't kill someone like that—"

"She was going to the next level, detective," Laura interjected. "I heard her running her spiel on the phone to a charity in Arizona. They help families with hearing-impaired children who can't afford the devices they need."

"She got the name from my list of charities that she found on the Internet," Joe added. "She was *relentless*. She went behind my back and, acting like *I* approved of it, she asked them for *half a million*! These were my people she was fucking with! *My people!* And they were very close to giving her the money! *Thank God* Laura told me about it so I could put a stop to it!"

Yeah. It was a ponzi scheme, Jane mused. Get half a mil from the next "investor," pay off the last group and use the rest for . . . "What was she was going to use the extra two hundred grand for?"

"She had it all figured out," Laura replied. "She told me she was going on a long trip. A two-month, first-class, cruise on the Mediterranean. Even though Joe put a stop to her stealing from the charity, I knew she'd find someone else to rob. No one ever told Carolyn 'no.'" Laura looked at Jane with pleading eyes. "Don't you see, Detective? She could go away on her cruise and never come home! And she would repeat the same criminal activities with someone else, in some other country. *Guaranteed.*"

"She basically needed to die. Is that what you're telling me."

"I think that's an excellent way to put it."

"Well," Jane said, "the guys back at DH are not going to believe this report when I write it up. It's not a whodunit. It's a who-didn't-do-it."

Laura stood up, supporting herself on the kitchen table. "*I did it*! I put the drugs in her drink! I wrote on her with the lipstick! I put those shredded promissory notes in her mouth and taped it shut! And I finished her off by taping up her nose! I killed Carolyn Handel! Arrest *me*!"

"Did you think that's how it was going to work when all of you conceived this promissory payback kill? Let Laura take the fall?" Jane looked at Joe. "That's not how it works, buddy. Everyone involved in this, including poor little Travis Wilde, is looking at conspiracy charges to commit murder. When a jury finds out that you're the sole beneficiary of your aunt's life insurance policy—" Joe suddenly stood up, reaching into his inside jacket pocket. Jane released her Glock and extended it toward Joe. "Hey!" Jane yelled. "Take your hand outta there!"

"I don't have a gun!" Joe screamed. "It's an envelope! You need to see it!"

Still training the Glock on Joe, Jane nodded. "Move slowly and toss the envelope to me."

He did as she requested, revealing a letter-sized white envelope. Jane recovered it, holstering her Glock. She opened the envelope and found three signed checks on Joe's personal account with no dates. There was one to Jacque Wilde, Charley P. Hall and Raymond Honeycutt, all for the amount of one hundred thousand dollars. "What in the hell?" Jane muttered.

"My aunt was worth three hundred grand dead. Exactly what she owed her investors. Somehow, I find that—"

"Ironic?" Jane suggested.

"Yeah. That's for real, Detective. And that was my altruistic intention from the very beginning. Now . . . how do *you* think a jury is going to feel about that one?" Joe's tenacious idealism suddenly reemerged. "And how about this: You have a twenty-eight-year-old guy who's dying from a heart defect, a down-on-his-luck, Vietnam vet who's a former P.O.W and a tortured man whose diabetes is literally eating him alive! Instead of being victims, they united against the oppressive tyranny and fought back! Oh, I think the jury is going to love that too! We're living in strange times, Detective. *Strange times*, indeed. The canyon between the haves and the have-nots is so wide, and it's growing. The natives have grown restless! You can smell revolution in the air. The old rules don't apply any more." He took a second and really looked at Jane. "And

I think you know that. I think you *truly* understand what I'm saying."

Jane couldn't argue with the guy. If he wasn't running a charity, he could have been a lawyer. Or a politician. Or the head of a commune. She couldn't argue but she still made all the arrests. The tentacles of revolution may be spreading, but they hadn't wrapped their limbs around this case. Not yet, at least.

CHAPTER 10

A week later, about ten o'clock at night, she got a call from Sergeant Weyler that Laura had been admitted to the hospital. She was informed that the woman who looked so old was dying of Stage IV cancer and would likely be dead within three months, long before any trial took place. One more thing to move the jury; one more irony for Jane to add to the list. Jane figured it was all part of the bigger plan—have Laura do the actual killing because if she got caught, what did it matter? She would find her freedom in death: both her own and that of her best friend.

But her freedom would come at the cost of vengeance. Vengeance is an odd bedfellow—at once, quietly cunning and then unflinchingly aggressive, fulfilling its duty to destroy that which it sees as a threat. Jane knew the beast. How many nights did she lie awake and plot the death of the one who tried to destroy her? How many times had she murdered him in her dreams? And what if she had actually shot him when she had the opportunity over twenty years ago? On that winter night, she was so close to pulling the fucking trigger. Would she have found a sympathetic jury who would cradle her and set her free or would she endure the harsh judgment of those who never experienced true evil at the hands of another?

"Evil requires the sanction of the victim," she thought again. He crept back into her consciousness. Jane lit her fourth cigarette of the hour and lay back on her bed while the darkness wrapped its familiar arms around her. She'd still be in its embrace when the sun rose.

CPSIA information can be obtained at www.ICGtesting.com
Printed in the USA
269008BV00001B/33/P